Shelley
the Sugar
Fairy

To Auriana and Elodie

Special thanks to Rachel Elliot

First published in the United Kingdom in 2017 as *Shelley the Sherbet Fairy* by Orchard U.K., Carmelite House, 50 Victoria Embankment, London EC4Y 0DZ.

ISBN 978-1-338-20725-5

10 9 8 7 6 5 4 3   18 19 20 21 22

Printed in the U.S.A.   40
First printing 2018

Shelley
the Sugar
Fairy

by Daisy Meadows

SCHOLASTIC INC.

Jack Frost's
Ice Castle

age

Animal Shelter

CHILDREN'S HOSPITAL

Community
Center

Children's
Hospital

Give me candy! Give me sweets!
Give me sticky, chewy treats!
Lollipops and fudge so yummy—
Bring them here to fill my tummy.

Monica, I'll steal from you.
Gabby, Franny, Shelley, too.
I will build a candy shop,
So I can eat until I pop!

Contents

An Extra Present

Rachel Walker was sitting at the bottom of the stairs in the house of her best friend, Kirsty Tate, fastening her party shoes.

"It's nice of your friend from school to invite me to her birthday party, too," said Rachel.

"Anna knows how excited I am to have you staying with me for a whole week," Kirsty said, smiling. "She's looking forward to meeting you."

Rachel jumped to her feet and smoothed down her party dress.

"I'm ready," she said. "Let's go."

Kirsty put their presents for Anna into a bag and then opened the front door. To her surprise, she saw her aunt Helen standing there.

"Oh!" said Aunt Helen. "How lucky—I was just about to knock. My goodness, you two look sharp!"

"We're on our way

to my friend Anna Goldman's birthday party," Kirsty explained.

"I know," said Aunt Helen. "Actually, I'm here to give you a ride to the party. You see, Anna has won a Candy Land

Helping Hands award, and I was hoping that you would present it to her."

Kirsty clapped her hands together in delight.

"This will be a really perfect birthday surprise for Anna," she said. "She has raised lots of money for the Wetherbury Children's Hospital."

Aunt Helen worked at Candy Land, a candy factory in town. She was in charge of organizing the Helping Hands awards, which were special gift bags of candy for local children who did helpful things around the community. Kirsty and Rachel had been helping her present the awards all week.

Kirsty and Rachel said good-bye to Mr. and Mrs. Tate, and then jumped into Aunt Helen's Candy Land van. It didn't take long

to reach the Wetherbury community center.

"Wow, the community center looks amazing," said Kirsty.

Rachel looked up. Colorful balloons were tied to the building's railings, and there were more around the doorway. A huge banner above the door said HAPPY

BIRTHDAY, ANNA!

"I'm good friends with Anna's mom," said Aunt Helen. "We got up early this morning and came here to decorate. I'm still shaking glitter out of my hair!"

The girls laughed as they got out of the van. Aunt Helen stayed in her seat.

"Aren't you coming in?" Kirsty asked.

"I'll be back soon," said Aunt Helen. "First, I'm going to Candy Land to pick up Anna's cake. Her mom told me that her favorite dessert is popping candy, so her Helping Hands award is a special popping candy birthday cake. I'll bring it here for the end of the party, and you can both help me surprise Anna."

As soon as the girls heard the words

"popping candy," they exchanged a
worried glance. Luckily, Aunt Helen didn't
notice. The girls waved good-bye as she
drove off. Then they walked up the path
to the community center, carrying the
bag holding their presents between them.

"I'd forgotten how much Anna likes
popping candy," said Kirsty in a low
voice. "I hope her cake isn't ruined by
Jack Frost and his terrible goblins!"

Candy had been going wrong ever since Jack Frost and his goblins had stolen the magical objects from the Sweet Fairies. Rachel and Kirsty had helped their fairy friends get three of the objects back, but there was still one missing.

Rachel looked down at the bag of presents and stopped in her tracks.

"Kirsty," she said in an urgent whisper. "Look at that!"

The bag of birthday presents was glowing as if a ray of sunshine was trapped inside. Feeling bubbly with excitement, Rachel and Kirsty peered inside. To their delight, they saw Shelley

the Sugar Fairy sitting on top of a sparkly birthday bow.

Shelley looked summery in her sunshine-yellow romper, with a beautiful pink rose in her brown hair. She fluttered out of the bag and flitted back and forth between the girls.

"Rachel and Kirsty, I have to get my magical packet of popping candy back from Jack Frost," she said in an urgent voice. "The Harvest Feast is today. Please, will you help me?"

Rachel and Kirsty exchanged a look of delight. They couldn't wait to help Shelley find her magical popping candy!

A Fizzy Mess

"We'll do everything we can," said Rachel.

On the first day of Rachel's visit to Wetherbury, Monica the Marshmallow Fairy had whisked the girls away to the Candy Factory in Fairyland. She had introduced them to Gabby the Bubble Gum Fairy, Franny the Jelly Bean Fairy, and Shelley the Sugar Fairy.

The Sweet Fairies had just invited the girls to the Harvest Feast when there was a commotion in the orchard. Jack Frost and his goblins were shaking candy off the trees. In the confusion, they stole four sparkly magical treats from the Sweet Fairies. Jack Frost wanted lots and lots of candy for the new candy shop at his Ice Castle, but instead of selling the candy, he was going to eat it all himself.

Without their special treats, the fairies couldn't make sure that all candy in Fairyland and the human world was sweet and delicious. Rachel and Kirsty had promised to help get them all back. They had found three, so now they just had to help Shelley get her magical packet of popping candy back.

Just then, the community center door started to open.

"Quick, hide in my bag," said Kirsty.

Shelley swooped into Kirsty's shoulder bag just in time. The door opened all the way, and a man came out carrying a bunch of balloons.

"Hi, Mr. Goldman," said Kirsty.

"Hello, Kirsty," said Mr. Goldman. "Please come on in. I'm just adding a few more balloons to the railings."

The girls walked in and saw balloons swirling in the air. Most of the children inside were jumping up and down, batting the balloons around.

"Look, there are the other Helping Hands award

winners," said Rachel.

Ori, Olivia, Tal, and a girl with blonde curls were bouncing around on hopper balls, giggling as they bumped into each other.

"Kirsty!" exclaimed the blonde girl.

She jumped off her hopper and ran over to hug Kirsty. Then she turned to Rachel.

"You must be Rachel," she said, smiling. "I've heard so much about you. I'm Anna. It's really great to meet you."

"Thanks for inviting me," said Rachel. "I love all the balloons! The food looks amazing, too."

There was a long refreshment table at the side of the room. The tablecloth was decorated with rockets, spaceships, planets, and shooting stars. There were enormous bowls filled with cookies, sour candy, and popping candy.

"My mom got lots of my favorite treats, but we're not allowed to eat them until later," said Anna. "I can't wait!"

Just then, the music stopped and Anna's mom clapped her hands together.

"It's time for the first game," she said. "Everyone gather around to play pass the parcel."

As soon as everyone was sitting in a circle, Mrs. Goldman started playing the music. A bulky package was passed around the circle, and when the music stopped, Rachel was holding the parcel. Eagerly, she ripped open the top layer and found a packet of popping candy.

"Oh yum, I love popping candy," she said. "Would everyone like some?"

She opened the packet and the popping candy fizzed right out, making a raspberry-colored mess on the floor.

"Oh no," said Rachel with a groan. "It looks like there is something wrong with the popping candy after all."

She exchanged a worried glance with Kirsty.

"I'll help you clean it up," said Kirsty,

jumping to her feet.

The girls wiped up the fizzy mess, talking in low voices.

"We can't let Aunt Helen bring the cake in here yet," said Rachel. "Not until we can find Shelley's magical packet of popping candy and take it back from Jack Frost and the goblins."

"We don't have much time," said Kirsty.

Just then, they heard a faint giggle. Then there was an excited squeal, followed by another giggle.

"It's coming from under the refreshment table," Rachel said.

The girls peeked under the tablecloth and saw four green, bumpy faces.

"Goblins!" they exclaimed.

Through the Keyhole

The goblins were cramming green popping candy into their mouths. Their cheeks were bulging, and popping candy was foaming out of their mouths and dribbling down their chins. The tallest goblin waved a popping candy packet, and a new pile of candy appeared in front of him.

Kirsty felt her shoulder bag move, and

looked down to see Shelley peeking out.

"That's my magical packet of popping candy," she said with an excited gasp. "Oh my gosh, I'm so happy that we found it—but I have no idea how we are going to get it back!"

The other children were still busy playing pass the parcel, and Mr. and Mrs. Goldman were watching the game.

"Let's go find a safe place where you can turn us into fairies," Rachel suggested. "Then we will have a chance to get close to the magical treat without the goblins spotting us."

"Yes, good thinking," said Kirsty. "How about the garden at the back of the community center?"

Rachel nodded, and Shelley ducked down inside the bag again. Then the girls

slipped out the back door and into the
garden. No one was watching, so Kirsty
opened her bag, and Shelley fluttered out.

"There's no time to lose," she said,
waving her wand.

"Jack Frost's goblins cannot scare me.
I'm a brave and fearless fairy!
Fly with me, do not delay.
We'll find the treat and save the day!"

A fountain of fizzing sparkles burst from Shelley's wand and showered the girls in sparkling fairy dust. They felt their skin tingling as they shrank to fairy size. Delicate pastel wings unfurled on their backs, and the sweet scent of candy filled the air. Rachel and Kirsty twirled upward, fluttering their wings in delight at being fairies again.

"Let's go back inside," said Shelley, taking their hands.

Now that they were small, they were able to swoop through the gap under the back door. They zoomed back into the

community center, flying high among the balloons and birthday banners. When they were above the refreshment table, they hovered and exchanged determined looks.

"Let's dive down and take the goblins by surprise," said Kirsty. "Maybe we can get the magical packet of popping candy before they realize what's going on."

Side by side, the three fairies whooshed under the tablecloth and flew toward the tallest goblin. He jumped up in a panic and banged his head on the bottom of the table.

"Fairies!" he squawked, staggering sideways. "Shoo! Go away!"

The other goblins scrambled away, stumbling over the candy they had dropped. One of them grabbed at the tablecloth and fell over. *CRASH!* The bowls of treats were pulled down from

the refreshment table, sending even more candy spilling onto the floor. The fairies peeked out from under the table. A green, fizzy mess was foaming across the floor toward the children, who giggled and jumped around when they saw it.

"They think it's another party game," said Kirsty.

"Poor Mr. and Mrs. Goldman," said Rachel.

Anna's parents were trying to clean up the mess, but it was getting worse.

"Where did the goblins go?" asked Shelley suddenly.

There was no sign of Jack Frost's helpers. Then Kirsty spotted some big footprints in the green, foamy mess.

"Those are goblin prints," she said. "Come on, if we follow them, they should lead us straight to the goblins—and the magical treat."

The fairies followed the footprints out of the community center's main room and across the hall toward a door labeled *Soft Play*. There wasn't a big enough gap under the door for them to get through, but Rachel pointed at the keyhole.

"We should be able to squeeze through there," she said. "It's made for an old–fashioned key."

She put her head into the keyhole and wriggled through.

Soft Play Party

When Rachel pulled herself out of the
keyhole, she heard the squeals, squawks, and
cackles of the goblins. They were jumping
around on spongy mats, a bouncy slide,
and a soft climbing frame. The goblin with
the magical packet of popping candy was
hurling brightly colored foam balls at the
others. Kirsty and Shelley popped through

the keyhole after Rachel.

"I think that the fizzy popping candy has made the goblins go completely fizzy with excitement," said Shelley. "I wonder if the tallest goblin will put my magical treat down while he plays."

The fairies watched the tallest goblin carefully, but he seemed to be clutching the candy packet more tightly than ever.

"How are we ever going to get it back?" Kirsty asked.

Rachel suddenly felt full of fizzy excitement herself.

"I have an idea," she said. "Maybe we can use those foam balls to make him drop the treat."

Together, the three fairies lifted one of the balls and aimed it at the goblin.

"Ready, set, GO!" said Rachel.

Together, they threw the ball at the goblin, but he dodged sideways and it missed. They flew down to get another

one, but they missed again.

"We have to keep trying," said Shelley, panting from the effort.

Over and over again, faster and faster, the fairies hurled the soft balls with all their might toward the goblin. But he was just too quick for them.

"This is fun!" he said, cackling with horrible laughter. "Is this what birthday parties are like?"

"I've always wanted to be invited to a birthday party," said another goblin. "Let me have a turn."

Kirsty turned to Rachel and Shelley.

"This isn't working," she said. "But I think I know what we should do. If these goblins want a party, let's give them a party. First, we will need to be human again. Then, we'll need a wrapped-up package and some music."

With a wave of Shelley's wand, Rachel and Kirsty were back to their normal size. A large package appeared in Kirsty's arms, and Rachel found herself holding the remote control for the stereo in the corner. Shelley quickly tucked herself into Kirsty's bag.

"Does anyone want to learn how to

play pass the parcel?" asked Kirsty in a loud voice. "It's one of the best birthday party games, I think."

Right away, three of the goblins raced over to her, jumping up and down in excitement.

"Sit down in a circle," said Kirsty, glancing at the fourth goblin, who was holding the magical packet of popping candy. "What about you? Aren't you going to join in the fun?"

"If I have to," said the goblin in a grumpy voice.

He joined the circle, still clutching

the magical treat in his hand. Rachel
and Kirsty sat down, too. Kirsty quickly
explained the rules, and then Rachel
pressed the PLAY button and the music
began.

The goblins
snatched the parcel
from each other
as they passed
it around, and
each held on
to it for as long
as they could.
When the music
stopped, the goblin who
was holding the parcel squealed with
excitement. He unwrapped the first layer
and found some green goblin stickers.

All the other goblins said "Oooh!" and

"Ahhh!" as they leaned over to see the stickers. The goblin clutched them to his chest, his eyes sparkling.

"This is the best game ever," he said.

The tallest goblin stared at the stickers in awe, but said nothing. The music started again, and next it was the shortest goblin's turn to unwrap a layer. Gleefully, he pulled out a pencil with a topper shaped like a goblin. The tallest goblin stared at it so hard that his eyes bulged.

Next, the music stopped on the tallest goblin's turn. He was so excited to find out what his prize would be that his hands were shaking. Rachel was sitting next to him, trying not to show that she was watching him out of the corner of her eye. Would the goblin let go of the precious candy packet?

Four Special Awards

The tallest goblin dropped the magical
packet of popping candy and started
to rip open the next layer of the parcel.
Rachel immediately picked up the treat
and handed it to Shelley. It instantly
shrank to fairy size, and Shelley tucked
herself into Kirsty's bag.

"Popping candy!" the goblin exclaimed

when he found his prize. "Yummy." He had already forgotten about the magical treat. While the goblins continued with their game, the girls slipped away and went back to Anna's party.

As they walked in, they could see that the foamy green mess on the floor had vanished. All the candy was back in the bowls, the tablecloth was back on the table, and the room looked clean and tidy again. Even the balloons were bobbing neatly in groups of red, blue, green, and yellow.

"It looks great in here!" said Rachel, and the other children nodded happily.

"Hey, everyone, guess what?" said Kirsty. "My aunt Helen is going to be here soon with a big surprise."

"Here she comes!" said Rachel, glancing out the window.

Shelley peeked out of Kirsty's bag, then hid again. A few seconds later, Aunt

Helen came into the hall, carrying a huge cake box. While Anna and all her guests sat down, giggling, the girls helped lift the cake out of the box. It had two iced layers, with stars and an enormous flying saucer on the top. Special candles spelled out Anna's name.

"It's perfect," said Kirsty.

They watched as Aunt Helen lit the candles. Then Rachel and Kirsty lifted the cake together and carried it toward Anna, singing "Happy Birthday." All the other children joined in. Anna's mouth fell open in amazement when she saw the incredible cake.

"This is a special birthday surprise from

Candy Land," said Rachel.

"You've been chosen to receive a Candy Land Helping Hands award!" Kirsty added. "They want to thank you for all your hard work, and all the money you have raised for the children's hospital."

"Happy birthday, Anna!" everyone cheered.

The rest of the Helping Hands award winners—Ori, Olivia, and Tal—gathered around Anna, hugging her and smiling.

"Congratulations, Anna," said Ori, smiling at her. "You really deserve it."

"I'm so honored," said Anna, with happy tears in her eyes. "Thank you. The cake looks incredible."

"How do you feel?" asked Mrs. Goldman.

Anna looked around at her friends' smiling faces, her pile of presents, and her wonderful cake.

"Getting presents and prizes is wonderful," she said. "But the best feeling comes from helping people."

"I agree," said Olivia. "Three cheers for Anna!"

All the children cheered as Anna went to cut the cake. Then each guest was given a slice.

"Yum," said Rachel after her first bite.

"It's delicious—and it even has popping candy in it!"

When the cake had been eaten up, Mrs. Goldman clapped her hands to get everyone's attention.

"It's time for a treasure hunt," she said.

"There are twenty packets of popping candy hidden in the back garden. It's your job to find them all."

Everyone charged toward the door. Giggling, Rachel and Kirsty ran to join in, but Shelley popped her head out of Kirsty's bag.

"Hold on," she said. "It's almost time for the Harvest Feast in Fairyland. Do you still want to come? Don't forget, time will stop in the human world while you're in Fairyland, so no one will notice that you've been gone."

Rachel and Kirsty held hands and exchanged excited smiles.

"We'd love to come," said Rachel.

Shelley waved her wand, and the girls disappeared in a flurry of magical sparkles.

The Harvest Feast

Rachel and Kirsty blinked as the sparkles faded. They were standing in the middle of the Candy Factory orchard in Fairyland, and it was filled with happy, busy fairies flitting to and fro. Long tables were set up around the orchard, laden with wicker baskets full of treats.

"It looks like the candy harvest went well," said Rachel with a smile.

"Everyone has been busy harvesting the delicious treats to get ready for today," said Shelley with a smile. "Oh look, there are the other Sweet Fairies. Monica! Franny! Gabby! I've gotten my magical packet of popping candy back!"

The other fairies zoomed toward
Shelley, Rachel, and Kirsty and threw
their arms around them, twirling around
in a big fairy hug.

"We knew that Rachel and Kirsty
could help," said a gentle voice.

It was Queen Titania. She and King
Oberon had appeared beside them. The
fairies fluttered apart and curtsied.

"We are delighted to have you here as our special guests," said King Oberon. "Thank you for helping the Sweet Fairies. We wouldn't be having today's feast if it weren't for you."

"We are so happy that we could help," said Kirsty.

The queen began to speak, but her voice was drowned out by a tremendous clap of thunder. Jack Frost appeared in a flash of blue lightning.

"How am I supposed to have a candy shop at my castle without any candy?" he demanded, jabbing his bony finger at Rachel and Kirsty. "It's all your fault!"

"You only wanted the candy so you could eat it all yourself," said Kirsty.

"Besides, you

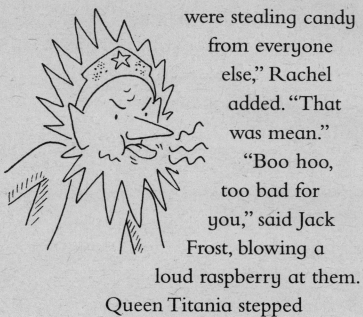 were stealing candy from everyone else," Rachel added. "That was mean."

"Boo hoo, too bad for you," said Jack Frost, blowing a loud raspberry at them. Queen Titania stepped forward, a serious look on her face.

"The Harvest Feast is supposed to be a happy and welcoming event," she said. "You were wrong to steal the magical treats, and you were wrong to be rude to our special guests. But if you can promise to behave yourself, we would like you to join our feast."

Jack Frost scowled, but then he saw all the candy in the baskets and nodded.

"Good," said King Oberon. "Then let the feasting begin!"

The Harvest Feast was one of the best parties that the girls had ever been to. Gabby held a biggest-bubble competition with bubble gum, Monica organized a marshmallow-on-a-spoon race, and

Franny ran a guess-the-jelly-bean-flavor competition. Rachel and Kirsty especially loved the fizzy party punch that Shelley made with popping candy. They laughed, played, and danced among the candy trees until the stars were twinkling in the sky. Then Shelley put her arms around their waists.

"I wish you didn't have to leave," she said. "But it's time for you to go and enjoy the other party now."

Kirsty and Rachel gave the Sweet Fairies one last hug good-bye, and then Shelley waved her wand. Suddenly, the girls found themselves running into the Wetherbury community center garden to join the treasure hunt.

"I'm glad we haven't missed a second of Anna's party," said Kirsty. "But I don't mind if we don't find any candy treasure."

"I agree," said Rachel, laughing.

"Candy is best as a special treat—and I think I ate enough in Fairyland!"

Soon it was time to go home. Anna gave the girls each a goody bag and a balloon as they left.

"Thank you for an amazing party," said Rachel, hugging her. "Happy birthday!"

In Aunt Helen's van, the girls peeked inside their goody bags.

"Yum, lots of popping candy," said Kirsty. "I'm going to share mine with Mom and Dad when I get home."

"Good idea," said Rachel. "I'm too full to eat any more candy today! Oh look, there's something else, too."

She pulled out a large packet of popping candy that said "Thank you" along the side, in glittery gold writing.

"How strange," said Aunt Helen. "I

helped Anna's mom fill the goody bags, and I don't remember putting those in."

Kirsty and Rachel exchanged a secret smile. They knew that it was a magical message from their fairy friends.

"I'm so glad we were able to help," said Kirsty in a low voice. "Now the Sweet Fairies can make sure that all candy is sweet and delicious. Didn't we have fun?

I wonder when we'll see our fairy friends again."

"Soon, I hope," said Rachel. "Having magical adventures makes me feel as fizzy as popping candy!"

THE SWEET FAIRIES

Rachel and Kirsty have found the
Sweet Fairies' missing magic items.
Now it's time for them to help

Robyn
the Christmas Party Fairy!

Join their next adventure in
this special sneak peek . . .

Crazy Crackers

"I've never seen frost look so beautiful," said Rachel Walker, gazing out the Town Hall window.

"It's a perfect Christmas Eve morning," agreed her best friend, Kirsty Tate, as she joined Rachel at the window.

The bright winter sun made everything outside the window sparkle. Kirsty's hometown, Wetherbury, looked as if it had been covered with glittery white icing. The girls and their families were spending Christmas there together this year.

"The party tonight is going to be amazing." Rachel smiled. "And helping organize it makes everything even more fun!"

She turned around, watching the preparations going on all over the hall. Lots of people from the community had come together to throw a special Christmas party. The girls and their families were thrilled! The food and decorations were looking wonderful, but the highlight of the party was definitely going to be a beautiful ballet performance.

Mrs. Tate saw the girls by the window and smiled at them.

"Come on, you two, there's work to do!" she said. "We have a lot to finish before the party. Could you start setting the tables for the feast?"

Several long tables had been pushed together to make a big square in the center of the hall. Mrs. Tate gave the girls a cart piled high with tablecloths, place mats, napkins, silverware, and glasses.

"Don't forget to put a Christmas cracker at each place setting," she said. "They're like party poppers, but they have small toys inside! The crackers are in a box on the bottom of the cart."

"I'm so excited about the Christmas party," said Rachel. "Just think, people all over the world are doing exactly the same thing we are right now—getting ready for Christmas."

"Not everyone!" said Kirsty. "At school, we've been learning about other holiday traditions from around the world, like Diwali and Hanukkah, and how people celebrate Christmas in all different countries."

The girls worked quickly, laying out the bright red tablecloths and beautiful place settings.

RAINBOW magic

Which Magical Fairies Have You Met?

- ❏ The Rainbow Fairies
- ❏ The Weather Fairies
- ❏ The Jewel Fairies
- ❏ The Pet Fairies
- ❏ The Sports Fairies
- ❏ The Ocean Fairies
- ❏ The Princess Fairies
- ❏ The Superstar Fairies
- ❏ The Fashion Fairies
- ❏ The Sugar & Spice Fairies
- ❏ The Earth Fairies
- ❏ The Magical Crafts Fairies
- ❏ The Baby Animal Rescue Fairies
- ❏ The Fairy Tale Fairies
- ❏ The School Day Fairies
- ❏ The Storybook Fairies
- ❏ The Friendship Fairies

📖 SCHOLASTIC

HiT entertainment

Find all of your favorite fairy friends at
scholastic.com/rainbowmagic

RMFAIRY17

RAINBOW magic ™

SPECIAL EDITION

Which Magical Fairies Have You Met?

- ❑ Joy the Summer Vacation Fairy
- ❑ Holly the Christmas Fairy
- ❑ Kylie the Carnival Fairy
- ❑ Stella the Star Fairy
- ❑ Shannon the Ocean Fairy
- ❑ Trixie the Halloween Fairy
- ❑ Gabriella the Snow Kingdom Fairy
- ❑ Juliet the Valentine Fairy
- ❑ Mia the Bridesmaid Fairy
- ❑ Flora the Dress-Up Fairy
- ❑ Paige the Christmas Play Fairy
- ❑ Emma the Easter Fairy
- ❑ Cara the Camp Fairy
- ❑ Destiny the Rock Star Fairy
- ❑ Belle the Birthday Fairy
- ❑ Olympia the Games Fairy
- ❑ Selena the Sleepover Fairy

- ❑ Cheryl the Christmas Tree Fairy
- ❑ Florence the Friendship Fairy
- ❑ Lindsay the Luck Fairy
- ❑ Brianna the Tooth Fairy
- ❑ Autumn the Falling Leaves Fairy
- ❑ Keira the Movie Star Fairy
- ❑ Addison the April Fool's Day Fairy
- ❑ Bailey the Babysitter Fairy
- ❑ Natalie the Christmas Stocking Fairy
- ❑ Lila and Myla the Twins Fairies
- ❑ Chelsea the Congratulations Fairy
- ❑ Carly the School Fairy
- ❑ Angelica the Angel Fairy
- ❑ Blossom the Flower Girl Fairy
- ❑ Skyler the Fireworks Fairy
- ❑ Giselle the Christmas Ballet Fairy
- ❑ Alicia the Snow Queen Fairy

▓ SCHOLASTIC
Find all of your favorite fairy friends at
scholastic.com/rainbowmagic

3 stories in each one!

HIT entertainment

RMSPECIAL20